D0230525

LANCASHIRE COUNTY LIBRARY

30118134758758

Disney
BEAUTY
AND THE
BEAST

BELLE'S TALE

By ERIC GERON

Screenplay by EVAN SPILIOTOPOULOS
and STEPHEN CHBOSKY and BILL CONDON

© 2017 Disney Enterprises, Inc. All rights reserved.

Scholastic Children's Books
Euston House,
24 Eversholt Street,
London NW1 1DB, UK

A division of Scholastic Ltd
London ~ New York ~ Toronto ~ Sydney ~ Auckland
Mexico City ~ New Delhi ~ Hong Kong

First published in the US by Scholastic Inc, 2017
Published in the UK by Scholastic Ltd, 2017

ISBN 978 1407 16579 0

Printed in Malaysia

2 4 6 8 10 9 7 5 3 1

All rights reserved

This book is sold subject to the condition that it shall not, by way of trade
or otherwise be lent, resold, hired out, or otherwise circulated without the
publisher's prior consent in any form or binding other than that in which
it is published and without a similar condition, including this condition,
being imposed upon the subsequent purchaser.

Papers used by Scholastic Children's Books are made
from wood grown in sustainable forests.

For more *Beauty and the Beast* fun, visit www.disney.com/beautyandthebeast

www.scholastic.co.uk

Lancashire Library Services	
30118134758758	
PETERS	JF
£4.99	09-Jun-2017
SKE	

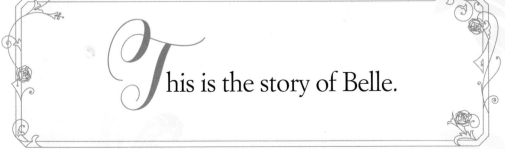

This is the story of Belle.

Belle was smart.

She loved to read.

Belle carried books everywhere.

She read about far-off places.

Like always, Belle bought bread from
the baker.

Every day was the same in the small village.
She longed for something more...

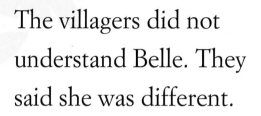

The villagers did not
understand Belle. They
said she was different.

Belle held her head high.
She was brave.

Belle was also kind.

She gave her bread and jam to a beggar.

Villagers saw Belle reading. They called her odd.

Belle tried to ignore the villagers.
But she wondered if they were right.

A man named Gaston also saw Belle.

Gaston was a rude brute. His best friend was LeFou.

Gaston thought Belle
was beautiful.

He wanted to marry
Belle for her looks.

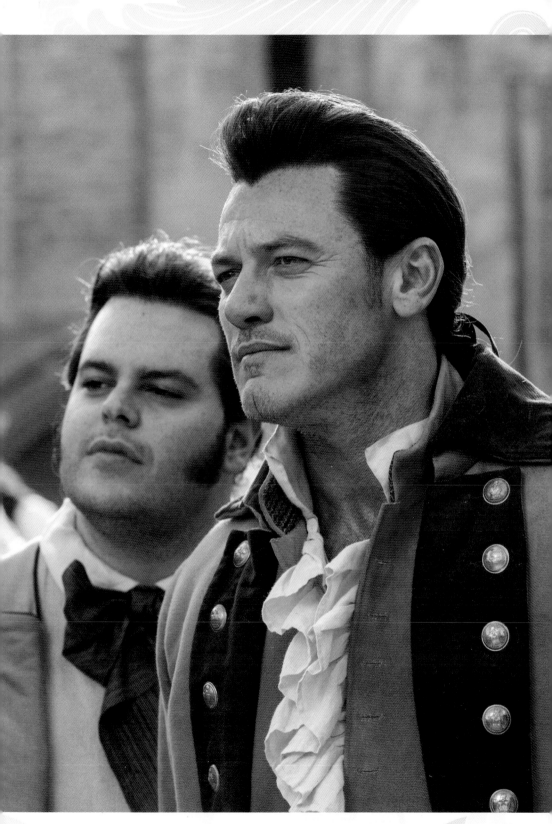

Gaston asked Belle to dinner, and Belle said no. He did not see Belle for her beauty within.

Belle hoped one day someone would understand her. She longed for something more...

Belle talked with her father, Maurice.
He told Belle that she was fearless and
daring.

Maurice told Belle to ignore the villagers. He loved that his daughter was different.

Belle loved her father very much. He
made her feel like she belonged.

He and his horse, Philippe, were leaving
for the market. Belle said goodbye to them.

The next day, Philippe
returned to the village.

Maurice was nowhere
to be found.

Philippe's reins were torn. Belle knew something was wrong.

She set out to find her father.

Clues led Belle into a strange castle.
She knew her father must be inside.

But she did not know what else she would find...

Belle was smart and brave and kind.
She soon found out the castle was
enchanted. Her fairy tale was about to
begin.